Iridium

H*use

By Emmy Scott

Written by Emmy Scott
Edited by Shannon Asplen
Watched over by Honey the pup

Special thanks to Shannon and Honey.
I couldn't have done it without you.
(Especially Shannon, you're the best)

Prologue

July

"But she can't be leaving me!" said Emmy sulking into a pillow.

Now while this sentence doesn't really make sense, it will soon. You see, Emmy is 10 years old and is going into year 7 at her new secondary school. But first we need to know how she got there.

"It's the last day of primary school!" screeched Emmy, running to Alice at the gate (they had been best friends since year 1).

"I couldn't wait, I told everyone!" exclaimed Alice.

"What?!"

"I found out everyones' new school! I'm going to Osmium High like everyone else, well except for a few Scandium House kids with powers, but still! Where are you going?"

"Iridium" said Emmy sadly. "But why are all the schools named after transition metals?"

"I have absolutely no idea, but we can still be friends! Plus, isn't that the school your brother goes to?" Alice asked.

"Thanks" said Emmy now slightly relived that she wasn't going to be alone on her first few years.

"We can still be friends until either of us finds new ones."

"Ok!"

A couple of weeks later Emmy receives a text message from Alice ...

Hey Emmy

Hi Alice

Remember what I said?

About what?

On the last day?

You said we could still be friends, right?

Yeh, so I made some new friends

So we won't be friends anymore?

Yeh

Don't text me anymore

Chapter 1

September

"And you've got your shoes, clothes, hat, uniform, coat, gloves, your toy dog, toothbrush, toothp-"

"Yes, yes, I've got everything" said Emmy in a rush. "Its not like I'll be gone forever, and I can call you if anything goes wrong!"

"Just not between 10 and 6 on Mondays and Thursdays because I'm busy so just text me."

"Ok mu-" Emmy looked at the time, it was 10:31 "WE ARE GOING TO BE LATE!!!"

Emmy grabbed her stuff and got into the car. Eventually her brother Johnny got in too, he was in year 10, and they started to drive to the station. They arrived just in time! Emmy said goodbye to her family and followed her brother to the train - she was about to get on when she saw girl about her age with all the luggage in the world and offered to help her.

"Thanks for helping me!" said the girl. She had long blond hair tied up in a ponytail and deep blue eyes. Emmy noticed she was wearing a cool band shirt with ripped jeans.

"You're welcome. By the way, I like your shirt!"

"Thanks. I'm Emma" said the girl.

"I'm Emmy."

"Isn't it cool that we have similar names!"

"Yeh, I hope that doesn't become confusing. Is that all your stuff or do you have like an evil twin called Sophie or something who makes you carry everything?"

Emma laughed. "You might not believe me, but you were exactly right with the second one."

"Even the Sophie part?"

"Even the Sophie part."

After a couple of second of giggles, a bright orange fox trotted over to their seats.

"Hey, guys do you mind if I sit here? There are no other seats" asked the fox, turning into a girl.

"Yes! Wait I mean no, yes, no... you can sit here" replied Emmy, now confused.

"Im Katrina" said the girl. She had long ginger hair tied loosely in low side ponytail. She was wearing an orange dress with a t-shirt underneath, with big black boots on her feet. She seemed chill.

"Im Emma and this is Emmy."

"Hi" whispered Emmy.

"What house are you going to be in?" asked Katrina.

"I'm in purple house," said Emmy.

"Yellow" said Emma.

"I'm orange house, I can turn into a fox." said Kat.

"I can manipulate molecules" said Emmy, showing off by making a little diamond from thin air.

"I don't have any powers, I'm pretty sure that all yellow house kids don't have powers," said Emma.

"I guess we will find out soon".

After 30 minutes they had arrived at Iridium House School. They were led to the lunch hall where they were assigned dorm rooms.

"Room G20! Ellie, Charlie, Kate Geralds, Pearl, Sharron Effarig, Sophie brown" said the headmistress, Ms McNugget. "Room G21! Amber Baker, Katrina Smith, Emma Brown, Rose Green, Luna Davis and Emilia Scott".

"Hey, I think we are all in the same dorm!" whispered Emmy to Kat and Emma. After a while the group of girls found their dorm room. They walked to another building where the dorm rooms were, and up to the second floor. Emmy, Kat, and Emma found their room and went inside. They stood there for a second when three girls walked into the small room...

The time was 11 pm, everyone was asleep, but something awoke Emmy. She opened her eyes and saw a strange light coming from underneath the bed. Creeping down the ladder, she pulled the cover off Amber.

"Hey" whispered Emmy "it's like...3am, put your phone away".

Amber rolled her eyes "Fine, also the time is 11:06".

"BEEP BEEP BEEP BEEP" shouted Emma "It's 6:32 and you should all be awake".

"Emma, it's too early for this, breakfast is at 8" whispered Emmy, struggling to get up.

"6:30 is a good time, plus what if we forget something".

"I miss my dogs," moaned Kat.

"And I miss my cat, but school starts in 2 hours 27 minutes, and we are going to be early" replied Emma. "Has everyone got their games kits?"

"Yes" replied Rose. "Now can we please go back to sleep?"

"Fine but don't blame me if you're late!"

At 8 o'clock the group sat together to eat breakfast.

"Hi" said Emmy sitting down at the table with her food. She looked at her bowl of Coco pops, toast, bacon, and glass of apple juice and licked her lips.

"Hi" said Rose.

"What are your classes this morning?" asked Amber.

"English then maths," said Emmy.

"Geography and maths" said Rose.

"English and maths," said Luna.

"French and maths," said Emma.

"BACON!" muffled Kat, through mouthfuls of bacon.

"I have English and maths," said Amber.

At break the group met up to have a snack.

"Hi" said Emmy.

"Where's Amber and Emma?" wondered Rose.

"I don't know," said Kat.

"Should we look for them?" said Luna.

It was now raining (probably due to Luna's frustration), and Amber was nowhere to be seen. They checked outside and there was Sophie and Emma. It looked like Emma was trying to grab Sophie's arm. When they looked closer, they could see Sophie trying to push Amber into the pouring rain...

SPLOOSH! "AAAAHHHH!"

"Amber are you okay!" shouted Emmy, running over to her. Amber's hair had turned murky grey in the rainwater.

"Amber are you okay?" asked Kat, worried.

"I'm okay, my hair just turns grey when its wet" said Amber, while Emmy was helping her up.

"We should go inside." said Rose, shielding her hair from the rain.

"Good idea," said Emmy.

"Why isn't my power working?" said Amber creating sparks from her hand.

"Maybe it's because your hair is linked to your powers? Maybe because it got wet your fire powers aren't working?" said Emmy, trying to hold a pencil between her lip and nose like a mustache.

"Yes, but my hair is almost completely dry, and my hair is still murky grey!" cried Amber.

"But what if your hair acts like lava? Then it makes sense that it doesn't go back to normal when its dry."

"Why does that make sense?" said Amber "Emmy?"

"Yes?"

"What are you doing with your hand?"

"Science."

"Im scared!"

"Does your hair feel hot?" asked Emmy, waving her fingers around in a purple glow.

"Why would I... oh my god it does feel warmer!" said Amber touching her head. "Emmy what did you do?"

"Like I said, SCIENCE!"

"Actually, what did you do? You can say science to anything."

"I moved around the particles around your hair really fast creating heat and congratulations your hair has turned normal again."

"Wow!"

"So how was your morning" asked Emmy, turning to Emma.

"Good!"

"Cool!"

"Cool."

"Nice."

"See you at lunch."

"Hi" said Emmy, looking exhausted after rowing.

 "Hi" said Amber, slumping down on her bed.

"Emmy?" said Emma.

"Oui oui mon ami."

"When did you last have a shower?"

"Sunday...last week."

"You need a shower. You smell like wet dog and Thames sock."

"No I don't!"

"Emilia Scott take a shower NOW!!"

"FIIIIIINE, but it's your fault if I get wet!"

"It's a shower, your supposed to get wet!"

"Ugh!" Said Emmy "SLAM!"

"EMMY! DON'T SLAM THE DOOR!!!"

"You are very annoying" shouted Emmy from behind the door.

"So how was your day, Amber?"

"Good!" said Amber cheerfully.

"Cool."

Chapter 2

October

"ITS HALLOWEEN!" screamed Emmy at the top of her lungs.

"Emmy, do you have any idea what time it is?" said Emma.

"Yes, its 6:30."

"Its 6:29, its too early!"

"Eh, same thing!"

"6:30 is the best time hands down" exclaimed Emma angrily.

"Heh but still, we need to think about the costumes, we only have 30 days!"

"We can decide at breakfast" replied Emma, half asleep.

"Fine!"

"Right, I've waited long enough for this" said Emmy siting at the table. "I've got a bucket hat and some paper and pens."

"Nice" said Rose.

Emmy reached her hand into the purple, shiny bucket hat and pulled out a piece of paper.

"Hamilton!"

"Emmy." said Emma, rolling her eyes. "How many pieces of paper say Hamilton on it?"

"7" said Emmy sheepishly.

"Should we pick another one?" asked Emma. Reluctantly, she reached her hand into the iridescent hat.

"Ugh...ghostbusters!" cried Emmy.

"Everyone OK about that?" asked Emma.

"Yes!"

There was an excited buzz around the table as everyone started to think about their potential costumes. Suddenly, a nervous looking girl carrying a tray appeared at the table.

"H-hi c-c-can I I sit w-with you, my r-roommates are i-ignoring m-me" said the girl with blond hair and grey eyes.

"Sure! I'm Amber, you might know me from class. This is Kat, Emma, Rose, Luna and Emmy, we were just discussing our Halloween costumes".

"I'm Puff" said the girl, sitting down.

"We're going as ghostbusters," said Emmy.

"That sounds really fun! I wish I could go trick or treating" said Puff sadly.

"You can come with us!"," said Rose, smiling.

"I wish I could, but the thing is, ... poison spikes shoot out of me when I get too scared" replied Puff, looking down at her tray.

"Well, we'll just have to make sure that doesn't happen! Now can everyone do Saturday at 12 at my place?" said Emmy.

"I think can make it at 1?" replied Kat.

"Ok cool."

The day was Saturday, and at 12 Emmy was looking out of the window.

"Hmm ... where is everyone?" said Emmy to herself.

Suddenly, there was a knock on the door. Emmy raced towards it - it was Luna and Rose.

"Hi" said Rose.

"Amber just texted me! She has to babysit her brothers!," said Luna.

"Oh" said Emmy, disappointed. She looked down at her phone. "Oh no! Emma and Kat can't come!"

"Why not?" said Rose.

"Kat has a football match, but Emma hasn't given an explanation," said Emmy.

"I guess we can do without them," said Luna.

Just then the doorbell rang. It was Puff.

"Hi, sorry I'm late" she said out of breath "there was way too much traffic."

"It's ok, should we go to my room" said Emmy.

The walls of Emmys room were light purple, and her decorations were purple to match. Lining the room were numerous draws, filled and labelled with different elements.

"Wow, your room is awesome!" exclaimed Luna.

"This is so cool. My room is just covered in pillows" said Puff, looking around in awe.

"My room is filled with plants," said Rose. She liked plants.

BUZZ BUZZ BUZZ

"Oh, it's my phone." said Emmy. "It's Amber!"

"Hi" said Amber over the phone.

"Amber, what happened" asked Emmy.

"I told my parents I was busy today, but they told me I had to babysit my brothers and sister. Ash! Take your finger out of your nose, you don't want to know what is in your snot! Annie don't eat playdoh, even though it looks like chocolate doesn't mean it is chocolate! Sorry, did I miss anything?"

"You didn't miss anything" said Rose reassuringly.

"OMG" said Luna "I was looking up kids' ghostbusters uniforms and I found one that might fit Kat".

"That is soooo cute, I love it" said Rose.

"Emma texted me!" screamed Emmy.

"What did she say?" asked Luna.

"I don't know, she used emojis."

"Then what are the emojis?"

"Cat, cat, cat, cat, cat."

"Is she talking about Kat?" said Rose, confused.

"If she was talking about Kat she would use foxes" said Emmy, resting her hand on her chin. She always thought better with her hand on her chin.

"Then what is she trying to say?" said Luna.

"I don't know" said Emmy typing back.

"It's probably to do with her cat. Annie, your little brother is not food, put him down!" said Amber.

"Well, I guess we will find out when we see her on Monday."

BUZZ BUZZ BUZZ

"That is my phone" said Luna "Hallo?... It's Emma"

"EMMA WHAT HAPPENED!!!" screeched Emmy, trying to look at the phone.

"Mr Muffins had six kittens" said Emma "I tried calling you, but you were on a call already!"

"WHO IS THE MOTHER!!!"

"Mr Muffins is the mother"

"Emma, I'm sorry to tell you but I think Mr Muffins might be a Mrs Muffins," said Luna.

"I knew that I was just never bothered to rename Mr Muffins, plus she now has a food bowl."

"So what are you going to do with them" said Rose.

"We could sell them, but I don't think anyone wants a tabby calico cat, so we might keep them because they are very cute."

"Wait if Mr Muffins is the mother then who is the father?" said Emmy.

"The father is most likely our neighbors' cat, Cookie Dough. Also, why are you asking so many questions?"

"I like cats, anyway this conversation went completely off topic, and we were supposed to be talking about the costumes. We found an absolutely adorable outfit for Kat!"

"Right, what'd I miss" said Kat plonking her stuff on her bed on Monday morning.

"We ordered the costumes and Luna's mum made us little name badges," said Emmy.

"And I'll bring the costumes next week," said Emma.

"Emma, I didn't know you wore jewelry!" said Kat looking at Emma's necklace.

"Yeh, it turns out Mr Muffins is a spirit animal and I'm her human."

"What's a spirit animal?" asked Amber.

"A spirit animal is basically an animal who has half their soul in an object like a necklace, but it's extremely rare" said Emmy.

"So how does it work?" asked Luna.

"I have no idea, but if the right person is wearing it then a projection of the animal shows and they can interact with it" explained Emma.

"Cool" said Kat.

On Halloween, the girls met up at Emmy's house.

"Before we sew on our name tags, I thought we should try on the costumes one last time" said Emmy handing them out to everyone. "Kat, you're the only one who hasn't tried yours on yet but I know you're going to love it."

"Emmy, why is mine so small?" said Kat in disgust, holding up the tiny costume in the air.

"We thought maybe you wanted to go as a fox?"

"This is for babies! The legs are too short and there isn't a hole for my tail."

"Give it to me" said Emmy, taking the outfit from Kat. She cut the bottom part off and sewed the edges.

"Now try it on."

"I feel stupid."

"That's the magic of Halloween"
cried Emmy, trying (and failing)
to hold back laughter. "You feel
stupid on the inside but
awesome on the outside. It also
looks really cute."

"I still hate it" insisted Kat.

"Wow these costumes are amazing," said Amber.

"Wait, wasn't Puff supposed to be here?" said Luna.

"'Apparently she had plans" said Kat.

BING

"Huh" said Emma, looking down at her phone.

"What is it?" asked Emmy.

"Sophie is with her. They are going to have a sleep over
at my house."

"Well, that was good timing but how do you know?" said Emmy.

"WhatsApp status."

"That stupid 'popular' girl with her stupid 'popular' friends" said Kat mocking them.

"Kat, she's my sister!" said Emma. "But that is a pretty good way to describe her" she said with a smile.

The girls got changed into their costumes and made sure they had everything they needed.

"Right, here's the plan. We split up in two groups. Me, Kat and Emmy will cover the even numbers and Luna, Amber and Rose will take the odd numbers. Then we will cross the street at 6:00 and meet back at 7:00 for the sleepover" said Emma. "Is that cool with everyone?"

"Let's do this!" said Emmy.

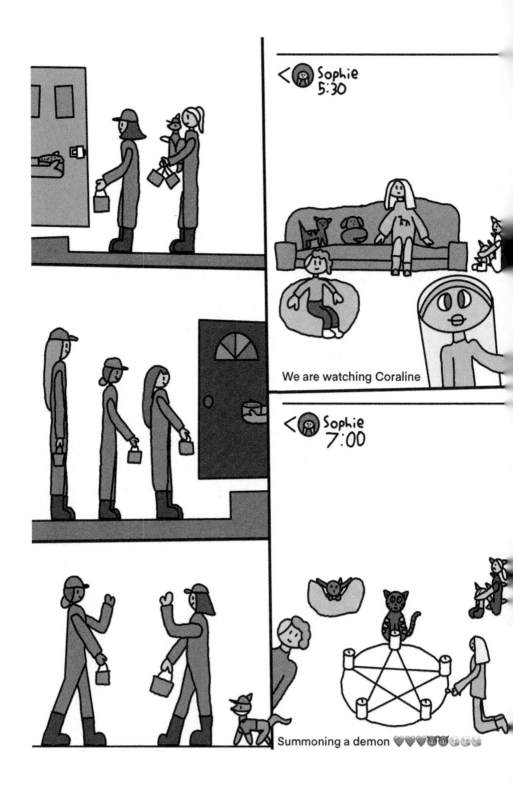

30

"How was trick or treating," said Amber.

"Good! I just checked my phone and Sophie is 'summoning a demon' or more appropriately, making friends, and look who it is, Miss 'I had plans' is with her," said Emma.

"Do you guys want to watch a movie before we go to sleep?" said Emmy.

"Sure!"

A bit later on (yes, I was too lazy and tired to draw anything).

"That was the BEST movie ever!" said Rose. "How have I not seen it!"

"I didn't like the scene where his son died but the music was so good," said Luna.

"Honestly it's good but the live action is way better" said Emmy.

"It sounds like my older brother playing Fortnite with his friends" said Amber holding back a laugh.

"Well, I'm going to bed" said Emma, holding back a yawn.

"Emma, don't you dare wake up at 6:30, it is a Saturday!" said Emmy.

"Ok fine, 7:00?"

Chapter 3

November

"Guten Montag"

"Emmy that means 'good Monday'" said Luna, laughing.

"I know."

"It's Sunday."

"Just get your butts off the sofa, I made French toast."

"Can I have..."

"Rose I got you some plain toast and Kat I got you bacon."

"BACON?" said Kat, excitedly jumping out of bed.

"BACON!!!" shouted Emmy.

"BACON IS THE BEST FOOD EVER!!!" screeched Kat running up from the basement to the kitchen.

"This french toast is AMAZING" said Luna stuffing her face.

"Hey, it's almost bonfire night" said Rose, taking a big bite of her toast.

"When is that?" said Emmy.

"You don't know 'Remember, remember the 5th of November'?"

"Isn't that Remembrance Day?"

"No" said Rose, looking at Emmy in astonishment.

"Emmy, it's hard to tell if you're extremely smart or extremely stupid" said Emma.

"Both"

(On Monday)

"PUFF!!!" screamed Emmy, running up to her at school.

"I-I'm so-so-sorry Sophie a-asked m-m-m-m-m-me a-a-and I-I made a mistake a-and-"

"That's it I'm murdering that Barbie rip-off."

"Umm Emmy, your eyes are going all purple and sparkly" said Amber...

Printed in Great Britain
by Amazon

23003534R00020